Judge Kim and the Kids' Court

The Case of the Missing Bicycles

written by **Milo Stone, Shawn Martinbrough,** and **Joseph P. Illidge**

illustrated by **Christopher Jordan**

Ready-to-Read *GRAPHICS*

Simon Spotlight

New York   London   Toronto   Sydney   New Delhi

SIMON SPOTLIGHT

An imprint of Simon & Schuster Children's Publishing Division
1230 Avenue of the Americas, New York, New York 10020
This Simon Spotlight edition August 2022
Text copyright © 2022 by Shawn Martinbrough, Milo Stone, and Joseph P. Illidge
Illustrations copyright © 2022 by Christopher Jordan
For information about special discounts for bulk purchases, please contact
Simon & Schuster Special Sales at 1-866-506-1949 or business@simonandschuster.com.
Manufactured in the United States of America 0722 LAK
2 4 6 8 10 9 7 5 3 1
Library of Congress Cataloging-in-Publication Data
Names: Stone, Milo, author. | Martinbrough, Shawn, author. | Illidge, Joseph, author. |
Jordan, Christopher (Illustrator), illustrator. Title: The case of the missing bicycles / written
by Milo Stone, Shawn Martinbrough, and Joseph P. Illidge ; illustrated by Chris Jordan.
Description: New York : Simon Spotlight, [2022] | Series: Judge Kim and the Kids' Court |
Summary: When bicycles go missing at Fairville Elementary School, it is up to nine-year-old
Kim Webster to listen to witnesses and evidence presented by her friends and settle the
case in her tree house court. Identifiers: LCCN 2021058819 (print) | LCCN 2021058820
(ebook) | ISBN 9781665919630 (paperback) | ISBN 9781665919647 (hardcover)
ISBN 9781665919654 (ebook) Subjects: CYAC: Graphic novels. | Courts—Fiction.
Stealing—Fiction. | Bicycles and bicycling—Fiction. | LCGFT: Graphic novels.
Classification: LCC PZ7.7.S755 Cas 2022 (print) | LCC PZ7.7.S755 (ebook)
DDC 741.5/973—dc23/eng/20220304
LC record available at https://lccn.loc.gov/2021058819
LC ebook record available at https://lccn.loc.gov/2021058820

Cast of Characters

Kim Webster

her little brother:
Miles Webster

their dog:
Digger

Miles' best friend:
Miguel

Kim's friends:
Ally, Simone, and Gabby

classmate:
Neil Strong

new kid at school:
Corey Boone

This is Kim. She's here to give you some tips on reading this book.

It's a beautiful morning in the town of Fairville.

Kim Webster and her dog, Digger, are still ound asleep.

Sometimes Kim has trouble getting up for school..

...but not today.

Kim follows the noise that interrupted her slumber.

Miles made it look so easy. But to Kim,
the tree house seems a million feet high.

Kim and Miles love riding their bicycles to school.

All the kids in Fairville pedal their bicycles to school.

Except for Neil Strong. His electric bicycle does the pedaling for him.

Kim hates seeing her friends fight.

Corey Boone is the new kid at school.

After school, the kids happily run outside to get their bicycles. But...

A short while later...

Welcome to the Fairville Courthouse! This is where Kim's mother works as a judge.

When people have a disagreement, they come to the judge for help.

She listens to both sides of the story. Then she looks at all the facts and evidence before deciding who is right and who is wrong.

Before her mom decides on the case, she wants to hear what Kim thinks.

At dinner Kim tells Miles about her day.

And then, Mom asked me what I'd do if I were the judge.

Judge Kim? That'll be the day!

I think Kim would make an excellent judge. She's smart, patient, and a good problem solver. Just like her mother.

Daddy, who could have taken my bicycle?

I bet Corey stole it.

We have a suspect. Why do you suppose it was him?

Kim considers Corey as a suspect, but it doesn't add up.

The next day at school...

Kim watches the ladder shake and sway.

You really think Corey stole my bike?

Uh-huh. Wouldn't you get tired of walking to school?

I guess I'm about to find out.

If you want to accuse Corey of stealing the bikes, you're going to need proof.

And how are we supposed to get that?

I think I know someone who can help.

WOOF!

Taking Kim's advice, the boys bring Digger to school to sniff for clues.

The boys follow the tracks through the country hills of Fairville until...

SNAP!

SLAM!

Corey, what are you hiding?

The next day at school...

Corey tries to explain, but the other kids won't listen.

Corey is a good kid. There must be more to the story.

Well, "Judge Kim," why don't you decide this case?

You know what? That's not such a bad idea!

Listen, everyone! If we work together, we can figure out the truth.

Kim gives each of her friends an im

Miguel, you go interview

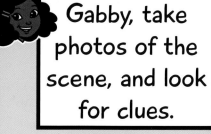

Gabby, take photos of the scene, and look for clues.

Simone, wear a disguise, and see what you can find at Corey's place.

Ally, you'll organize the evidence that everyone gathers.

The Kids' Court will soon be in session!

But where...?

Climbing up to the tree house seems just as scary as ever. But Kim knows she can make the climb...

...if she takes it one step at a time.

Up the ladder Kim goes, never looking down.

Gosh, that wasn't so scary after all.

I can see all of Fairville from up here!

And this will make the perfect courtroom!

One by one the kids all get a chance to speak.

When we discovered our bikes were missing, Corey was the only kid that wasn't with us.

The school janitor said Corey left early that day.

Corey stole the bikes so he wouldn't have to walk to school anymore.

Things aren't looking good for Corey.
The evidence against him is piling up.

However, Kim knows that Corey deserves a
chance to defend himself before she decides
on the case.

Gabby! You got your bike back?!

Yes! I found it parked in front of my house.

Best of all, it has a brand-new paint job!

The kids gather back inside to hear Corey's explanation.

Corey?

My dad is a mechanic, and I watch him fix things.

I thought I could make new friends at school by fixing their bikes.

So I took the bikes when nobody was looking.

I fixed them using recycled parts.

I even added some fancy upgrades.

I'm sorry.

Kim thinks about everything that was presented. Now it's time for her to decide, who was right, and who was wrong?

Outside, Corey's brother arrives with a surprise.

Kim writes in her journal about climbing scary ladders, the missing bicycles, and her very first time as a judge.

It turns out that getting over my fear of heights ended up helping my friends, too.

P.S. I can't wait to ride my *bike* to school tomorrow.

Justice is done...until the next exciting case for Judge Kim and the Kids' Court!

GLOSSARY

case: a disagreement between two people or groups that is decided in court.

court: a place where a judge listens to and decides on cases.

evidence: information presented in court to help a judge understand a case.

judge: a person who listens to cases and decides who is right and who is wrong.

justice: when a proper punishment or fair treatment is given by a judge.

motive: the reason a person did something or acted in a certain way.

suspect: a person who is believed to have done something wrong.

witness: a person who saw something happen that is related to a case.

Note to readers: Some of these words may have more than one definition. The definitions above match how these words are used in this book.